Little Tim books
by Edward Ardizzone

published by HarperCollins*Publishers*

TIM'S FRIEND TOWSER

by

Edward Ardizzone

HarperCollinsPublishers

For my Grandson, Quentin

Tim's Friend Towser
Copyright © 1962 by Edward Ardizzone
Printed in Belgium. All rights reserved.
www.harperchildrens.com

First published in 1962 by Oxford University Press.
Reissued in hardcover in Great Britain by Scholastic, Ltd., 2000,
and in the United States by HarperCollins Publishers in 2000.
Published by arrangement with the Estate of Edward Ardizzone.

Library of Congress Cataloging-in-Publication Data
Ardizzone, Edward.
  Tim's friend Towser / by Edward Ardizzone.
      p.   cm.
  Summary: Tim and Ginger, cabin boys on the S.S. Royal Fusilier, adopt a stray puppy and decide to
hide him aboard ship out of sight of the captain who hates dogs.
  ISBN 0-688-17677-1
  [1. Dogs—Fiction.   2. Sea stories.]   I. Title.
PZ7.A682 Tip   2000   00-20137
[E]—dc21   CIP
                                                                                 AC

1 2 3 4 5 6 7 8 9 10
❖

Tim and Ginger were cabin boys on the S.S. *Royal Fusilier* with Captain Piper in command.

Their first day at sea was a stormy one. The sea was rough, and, though it was cold, Tim and Ginger paced the deck in order to get a breath of fresh air.

Above the whistling of the wind they heard a strange little noise coming from one of the boats.

Ginger thought it was the crying of a seagull, but Tim said, "Nonsense, it is quite

different from that." So Ginger climbed up and looked into the boat.

In the boat was a tiny puppy. It was squeaking and squeaking because it was cold and hungry.

Now Captain Piper loved cats, especially his cat Tiger, but he simply hated dogs and heaven knows what he would do to one, even if it was only a puppy, if he found it on board.

"Poor little thing," thought Tim. "We can't let the Captain see it." So he and Ginger decided there and then to hide it in their cabin and, when the ship stopped at the next port, they would take it ashore and try and find a home for it.

Tim found an old cardboard box in which he put his second best jersey and so made a nice warm bed for the puppy. He kept the box under his bunk.

They fed the puppy with food which they saved from their meals. They would put a little bit of meat or a piece of bread and butter in their pockets and hurry down to the cabin to feed it.

It was a greedy puppy and always ate the food up.

When they had no work to do they spent the time in their cabin playing with it.

They called it Towser.

At the first port at which the ship stopped Tim smuggled Towser on shore under his jersey. But though he asked everybody he met, none of them would give the puppy a home.

This happened again at the next port and the port after that and so on and so on. Nobody would have it.

"Oh dear!" thought Tim. "What are we to do?"

And so the weeks went by and the problem became worse and worse, because Towser grew bigger

and bigger

and bigger.

So big that he had to be smuggled on shore in a kitbag, and the bigger Towser

became the less chance there was that anybody would want him.

Also, as Towser became bigger he became hungrier and hungrier and though Tim and

Ginger asked for second helpings of everything, they ate less and less themselves and left the table with their pockets simply bulging with food.

In fact, as Towser grew bigger and bigger,

Tim and Ginger became thinner

and thinner

and thinner.

I'm so hungry I could eat a horse.

This made the cook very cross. "Drat the boys!" he said. "I give them more and more good food and they only get thinner and thinner. Something must be wrong with them. They need a tonic." So three times a day after meals he dosed them with very nasty medicine.

However worse was to happen.

Tim and Ginger would take turns giving Towser a walk on deck after dark. There was little danger of them being seen by any member of the crew, as the few on deck were busy keeping the night watch. The real danger came from the Captain who liked to pace the bridge at all hours. So Tim or Ginger would keep Towser as far away from the bridge as possible.

Unfortunately Towser would sometimes slip his lead and escape.

One night the Captain was on the bridge with Tim.

"Tim," he said, "there's a dog over there on the poop deck. Can you see it?"

"No sir," said Tim, keeping a straight face, though he could really see Towser quite well.

A few nights later the same thing happened again, but Ginger was with the Captain this time.

"Ginger, there's a dog on board and I won't have dogs on my ship. Can you see it?"

"No sir," said Ginger.

"Strange," said the Captain. "I must have imagined it."

Now this happened over and over again until the Captain became terribly worried. He was always seeing dogs which nobody else could see and he hated dogs. Perhaps he was sick? Perhaps he had brain fever? He felt sure it was something very bad indeed, so he shut himself up in his cabin and sulked and sulked.

His only real companion was Tiger the cat.

In fact, because of Towser, the ship became an unhappy one.

The Captain sulked in his cabin; the First Mate was worried because the Captain would not give any orders; the cook was cross; and the crew slacked because nobody seemed to be in command.

Then the weather grew worse.

A great gale started to blow from the West, where the worst storms come from. The S.S. *Royal Fusilier* was a gallant ship, but with a sulking Captain and a slack

crew she wallowed in the waves like a piece of old driftwood.

An enormous wave came over the side and smashed part of the forward hatch cover and water poured into the ship.

The First Mate dashed into the Captain's cabin and told him what had happened, but all the Captain would say was, "Go away and don't bother me."

"I'm frightened," said Ginger. "If this goes on the ship will sink."

"I'm frightened too," said Tim. "Quick, let's go and tell the Captain the truth about Towser and then perhaps he might stop sulking and take command. Oh dear! Oh dear! I wish we had done this before."

The wind was so strong and the ship rocked so much, that it was only with the greatest difficulty that Tim and Ginger made their way onto the bridge and into the Captain's cabin.

"Go away," roared the Captain in a terrible fury.

"Please sir," said Tim, "there really is a —" But he got no further than this, for at that moment there was a fearful din of hissing, spitting, growling and barking, and into the

cabin rushed first the ship's cat and after him Towser. They dived under the table.

"ZOUNDS!" said the Captain, who sometimes used strange words. "ZOUNDS! I have been bitten by a ghost!"

Towser had bitten his leg by mistake.

But the Captain soon found that it was
not a ghost, because he had had a real bite
which was bleeding like anything and there
in front of him was a real dog.

He realised then that he was not mad
after all.

"What's wrong with the ship?" he
shouted, as it gave another terrible lurch.
Then he dashed onto the bridge and took
command. He was his old self again.

The Captain ordered the Engineer to make the engines go slower, the man at the wheel to alter course, the pumps to be started and all hands on deck to mend the hatch cover.

This was a dangerous and difficult task because great waves often dashed over the side.

Tim and Ginger were told to go below to

the galley, as they were small and might easily get washed overboard.

They were also told to take Towser and the cat with them.

The galley was in a terrible mess. The stove was out; everything had fallen off the shelves; pots and pans, packets of salt and bags of sugar were floating about in a foot of sea water, which washed backwards and forwards across the floor.

Tim and Ginger, Towser and the cat climbed on top of the bread locker and sat there feeling cold, wet and miserable.

Now a curious thing happened. As time went by, Towser and Tiger the cat made friends.

Towser licked Tiger and Tiger purred. Tiger licked Towser who looked quite pleased and did not even give a little growl.

After what seemed hours and hours the ship rocked less and there was less water on the floor.

Suddenly the door was flung open and in came the cook.

"Boys," he said. "The Captain wants to see you and the dog."

Poor Tim and Ginger. They were more frightened of the Captain than they had been of the storm.

The Captain was furious and called them bad boys and Towser a vicious animal.

Tim tried hard to explain but could not get a word in edgeways.

At that moment in walked Tiger. Instead of jumping on the Captain's knee which he usually did, he rubbed himself against Towser and purred and purred.

The Captain was astonished at this and seemed less angry. But all the same he said that Tim must put Towser ashore at the next port and leave him there, even if he could find nobody to take him.

After the storm the weather became fine and the S.S. *Royal Fusilier* sailed across a calm blue sea.

The sailors were busy on deck repairing damage and hanging up their wet clothes to dry. All were happy to be alive and well.

But Tim and Ginger were unhappy. They knew it would not be long before they reached a port and they would have to say goodbye to Towser for ever.

Nevertheless, though they were unhappy, they put on weight, because now the cook fed Towser they could eat up all their meals.

Towser seemed to guess that these were his last days on board and was on his best behaviour.

He played with Tiger and never chased him.

He kept out of the Captain's way and he made friends with the crew.

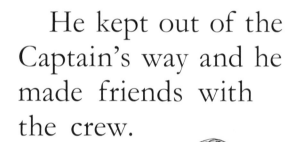

His particular friend was the cook, who became very fond of him.

The Captain still seemed cross but this was for quite another reason. He was annoyed because Tiger spent most of the time playing with Towser instead of sitting with him in his cabin as he used to do.

The truth was the Captain was rather jealous.

At last the sad day arrived when the
S.S. *Royal Fusilier* steamed slowly into the
harbour of a small seaside town.

The crew had put on their best clothes

and were waiting anxiously to disembark. They looked forward to being on dry land again. Tim and Ginger had also put on their best clothes.

They had given Towser a good brushing
and had tied a red ribbon on his collar to
make him look as smart as possible.

Would they find somebody to give
him a home? They felt there was little
chance now.

Soon the ship arrived alongside the quay. Tim, Ginger and Towser had been waiting patiently on deck. Now they prepared with heavy hearts to go down the gangway.

Many of the sailors had come to say goodbye to Towser, but he looked more miserable than ever.

They had hardly started down the gangway when they heard a shout. It came from the cook.

"Hey! Boys!" he said. "Wait a bit. The crew and I are going to see the Captain about this."

Then all the sailors gathered together in front of the bridge, and shouted "WE WANT TOWSER."

"Very well," said the Captain. "He seems a nice dog and Tiger my cat likes him. You can keep him."

"Hurrah!" shouted the crew. "Hurrah!" shouted Tim and Ginger.

"Wuff, Wuff!" barked Towser.

After this, Towser became great friends with the Captain and he and Tiger would spend much time with him in his cabin.

But always Towser liked Tim and Ginger best.

— *The End* —